HERCULES: NEW PUP ON THE BLOCK

Peter Clover

Galaxy

CHIVERS PRESS
BATH

First published 2000
by
Hodder Children's Books
This Large Print edition published by
Chivers Press
by arrangement with
Hodder Children's Books
2001

ISBN 0 7540 6162 0

British Library Cataloguing in Publication Data
Clover, Peter
    New pup on the block.—Large print ed.—(Hercules;1)
    1. Hercules (Fictitious charcter) 2. Dogs
    3.Children's stories 4. Large type books
    I. Title
    823.9'14[J]

ISBN 0-7540-6162-0

Printed and bound in Great Britain by
REDWOOD BOOKS, Trowbridge, Wiltshire

HERCULES: NEW PUP ON THE BLOCK

It's Jack's birthday. A puppy is all he's ever wanted. But Hercules is a huge disappointment. Short, squat and funny, but not what Jack had in mind. There's no going back though. Ignoring this scruffy bundle of fur is his only option. But Hercules is a dog who won't give up. Even when Jack leads him into terrible danger . . .

For Little Boy Blue

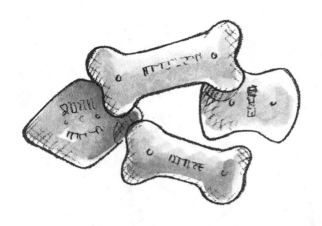

CHAPTER ONE

It was a brilliant, sunny Saturday afternoon. And, as usual, the little seaside resort of Fentown was busy and bustling with happy holidaymakers.

Jack Singer peered through the gleaming glass door of the new pet shop. At first he saw only his own reflection: a small, fair-haired boy in faded blue jeans and a white T-shirt. Then he saw the puppy inside and his eyes grew wide with excitement. Jack soon forgot all about the bus he was waiting for and leaned forward,

pressing his nose against the door for a better look.

At the counter, a man was busy buying dog-biscuits and squeaky toys. A young girl stood next to him with a new puppy on a lead. The puppy flopped down on the floor and gave both its ears a good scratch. One pink nose twitched. And two big brown eyes stared back in wonder at the face pressed against the glass.

'You're so perfect,' murmured Jack. He smiled at the tiny black puppy and tapped his fingers against the door. The puppy cocked its head to one side and flicked up its ears. Jack wished he

could have a puppy just like it. He read a card in the window: GOOD HOMES WANTED FOR CROSSBREED LITTER. YARNER FARM. And it gave the number. Jack was just fumbling for a pen in his backpack when he heard the bus turn into the street. Sighing, he gave up the search.

Jack climbed up on to the yellow hopper shopper, paid the driver his fare and sank back into a window seat.

As the bus left Fentown and set off home along the country lanes to Sallyford, Jack found himself daydreaming about his own perfect puppy.

By the time the bus pulled up at Jack's stop, he had already named his puppy. He was going to call it Wolf.

Wolf would grow into a big, strong, fearless dog and Jack would teach him all kinds of brilliant tricks. Wolf would be the cleverest dog in the whole universe.

Jack ran happily down the lane calling Wolf to heel. He picked up a stick and threw it for the imaginary dog to chase after.

'Fetch, Wolf. Fetch! Good boy, Wolf. Sit! Attaboy, Wolf.'

As Jack passed the railway station, he hopped over the low picket fence and made his way across the iron bridge to platform one, on the other side.

Jack's dad was the station manager at Sallyford. And every morning and afternoon he took the *Pacific Princess* out on its two daily excursions along the coast. The old steam engine was always busy ferrying tourists between Sallyford and the two seaside towns of Fentown and Rilport. It was a very popular trip with the holidaymakers.

Jack glanced at the station clock. It was half past four and the *Pacific Princess* was due back from its last run at any minute.

Jack was going to tell Dad all about Wolf on the way home to the cottage. And by the time they'd reached the front gate, Dad would have agreed to get Jack a puppy of his own.

Well, that was Jack's plan anyway.

* * *

Mum was laying the kitchen table for tea. Jack was upstairs washing his hands. The smell of Tiddlers' Delight filled the cottage. Sausage casserole with carrots and dumplings. The Tiddlers were a tin of baked beans added at the very end.

Mum tipped in the beans and gave the casserole a final stir.

'What kind of dog is it he wants?' she asked.

Dad shrugged his shoulders. 'He didn't say. All I know is that he saw a girl with a puppy in the pet shop. And now Jack has his heart set on one.'

Mum spooned the casserole on to plates and smiled at Dad across the kitchen table.

'It's Jack's ninth birthday next week. I bet he'd just love to have a little puppy.'

They decided there and then that Dad would visit the rescue kennels out at Crossmead, first thing on Monday, after his morning shift, and find out about adopting a dog for Jack. A puppy just like the one he'd seen in the pet shop.

*   *   *

A week later, there was a surprise waiting for Jack when he came home from school.

Mum and Dad were both sitting in the kitchen. Jack thought there was something funny going on the moment he stepped through the door, because neither of them were doing anything. They were just sitting there, grinning.

Jack quickly glanced around the room. He half expected a visiting aunt to leap out from one of the kitchen cupboards, and smother him with kisses. They both had that sort of look about them; as though something funny was about to happen at any moment.

Jack found himself grinning, too.

'What is it?' Jack asked. 'What's happened?'

Mum was the first to speak. 'We've got a nice surprise for you, Jack.'

Jack's face lit up immediately, just like a Christmas tree.

'A birthday surprise,' added Dad.

7

'But it's not my birthday until Wednesday,' said Jack.

'We know. But your present has arrived two days early this year.' Mum and Dad smiled at each other.

Jack was so excited, he was hopping about on the spot, jumping from one foot to the other.

'Is it Wolf?' he asked. 'Is it my puppy?'

By now, Jack was almost certain that it was.

'Well . . . he's hardly a puppy,' smiled Mum. 'He's upstairs in your room.'

'He was a rescue dog up for adoption. His name is—' But before Dad could finish, Jack was bounding up the stairs, two steps at a time.

Jack peered into his bedroom. His heart was thumping in his chest. He had never felt so excited in his life. He could hear Mum and Dad clomping up the stairs behind him, and quickly looked around the room for Wolf. But there was no sign of a puppy anywhere.

Then Jack noticed a slight movement behind his duvet. Right down by the side of the bed, where the cover touched the floor. The duvet was being poked and pushed from behind.

Jack's eyes grew as large as saucers as a little black nose appeared. Then his mouth dropped open in surprise as a scruffy grey head poked its way out through the folds.

Two very bright eyes sparkled beneath a wiry, scrubbing-brush fringe. They looked straight at Jack. And Jack

stared straight back in horror as the dog crawled out of his hiding-place.

It seemed to take for ever. This dog was so *long*. It seemed as though it was unwinding itself from a big reel hidden somewhere under the bed.

It didn't seem to have any legs, either. Its long hair almost brushed the ground when it walked.

'What's *that*?' cried Jack. 'That's not Wolf! That's not my dog.'

'His name's Hercules,' said Dad as he walked into the room. He could see that Jack was quite clearly disappointed.

'Hercules,' said Jack, bitterly. 'How can you call a dog like *that* Hercules? It looks more like a sausage. It's as fat as a sausage. And it's probably more *use* as a sausage.'

And, with that, Jack pushed past his father, thundered back down the stairs and stormed out into the front garden.

CHAPTER TWO

'Oh, dear!' said Mum, coming into the room to join her husband. 'He really doesn't like Hercules, does he? I suppose he's nothing like the puppy Jack saw in the pet shop.'

'Well, no,' said Dad. 'But they didn't have any puppies at the rescue kennels. We can't take him back now. We've been vetted by the RSPCA and I've signed all the papers. I've promised to give Hercules a good home. I thought Jack would love him. Just look at those bright, intelligent eyes!'

At this, Hercules cocked his head to one side, listening to every word. This little dog understood quite a bit about humans.

Hercules lay on the rug in the middle of Jack's room with his head on crossed paws, and made his eyes look wide and innocent.

'No! We definitely can't take him back,' said Dad. 'It wouldn't be fair. A dog is for life. Jack will just have to get used to him. Hercules is here to stay!'

*　　*　　*

Jack was in the front garden kicking at the gravel path with the toe of his trainers. His bottom lip was sticking out and he was sulking.

Hercules! he thought. *What a stupid name to give such a titchy dog. Stupid dog anyway.*

Just then, Hercules appeared and dropped a ball at Jack's feet. The little dog's tail waggled about as though it were on a spring.

Jack ignored the ball and moved away. Hercules picked it up and

12

dropped it at Jack's feet again. This time Jack kicked the ball in a temper, and the little dog flew after it like a rocket.

Hercules brought the ball back and once again placed it in front of Jack.

Hercules sat staring up at his new young master with the most appealing look he could manage. Bright eyes twinkling. Ears perky and alert. Tail thumping the ground. He even raised one front paw and paddled the air with a doggy wave.

'It's no use. I'm NOT playing.' Jack sounded really grumpy. Not at all like the happy, cheerful boy he was normally.

Hercules nudged the ball with his nose and pushed it right between Jack's legs.

'I TOLD you, I'm NOT playing,' Jack almost shouted.

Then he picked up the ball and threw it as hard as he could. The ball sailed over the privet hedge and out into the lane.

'*Owww!* Who threw that?'

CJ was walking down the lane on her

way home from school. CJ's real name was Caroline Jones. She was one of Jack's friends from school and a real tomboy. The ball bounced off her head and came back over the hedge.

Hercules took an incredible flying leap and caught the ball just as CJ passed the gate and peered over into the garden.

'What was that?' said CJ rubbing her head. 'A circus trick?' She looked at Hercules and screamed with delight. 'Whose dog is *that*? It looks cool. I bet it's a real laugh.'

'It's mine,' mumbled Jack. He looked down at the grass. Jack was still sulking and determined not to be won over by the hairy charmer at his feet. Even though Hercules was now rolling on his back and showing off his pink belly.

'What's his name?' asked CJ.

Jack screwed his mouth tight. 'Hercules,' he muttered.

CJ spluttered with laughter. '*Hercules!* That's brilliant! It suits him down to the ground, doesn't it? The little hero with the big name!'

'Hero!' said Jack. 'What do you mean, *hero*? He hasn't done anything yet. He's just a short, fat zero!'

'You say that *now*,' winked CJ, 'but I bet you two are going to be the very

15

best of friends.'

Jack said nothing; just watched as CJ strolled off home.

Without even glancing at Hercules, Jack picked up the ball and stuffed it deep into the pocket of his jeans. Then he went straight back to his sulk and continued kicking at the gravel path with his toe.

Hercules ran off for a second, then reappeared with something clamped between his jaws. He dropped his find on the ground beneath the privet hedge, then began digging for all he was worth in the soft brown earth. Clumps of mud and dirt went flying everywhere, and at last a big hole appeared.

Jack couldn't resist glancing sideways to see what Hercules was up to. Then he saw it.

'My best baseball cap!' yelled Jack. And the chase was on.

Round and round the front garden they raced. Through the flower borders and in and out of the rhododendron bushes. Down the side of the cottage to the backyard, then round to the front again.

Jack almost caught up by the old apple tree, but Hercules was far too fast for him.

Mum and Dad were watching all this from a downstairs window.

'It looks like they've made friends,' said Mum.

'I *knew* it wouldn't take long,' Dad smiled. 'There's nothing quite like a boy and his dog, is there?'

'You'd never think that such a little dog could run so fast, would you?' said Mum, as Hercules and Jack tore past the window. 'He's like a rocket.'

Outside, the atomic Hercules shot round the cottage to the backyard again. Only this time he allowed himself to be cornered between Dad's tool-shed and the plastic rain barrel. It was obvious to Hercules that Jack was never going to catch him.

'Right! Gotcha now!' growled Jack. He was very red in the face, and puffing and panting like the old *Pacific Princess* steam engine.

Hercules sat up on his haunches, begging. Jack's baseball cap dangled

17

from his mouth. Hercules had been very careful not to damage it. Jack snatched the cap away and Hercules gave a little whine.

'I'm sorry,' said Jack, pulling the cap down firmly over his hair. 'It's not your fault. I'm sure you're a nice dog really, but you're just not the dog I wanted.'

Jack turned the cap's peak to the back of his head and walked away. He could hear Hercules whining, but he didn't look back.

Jack felt rotten but he just kept walking, and went into the cottage for his tea.

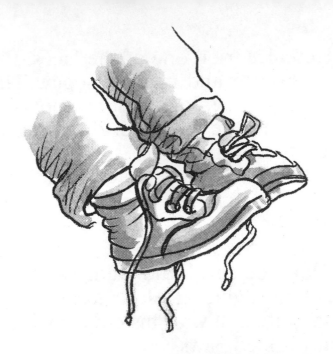

CHAPTER THREE

Hercules lay underneath the kitchen table peering through a sea of legs. The wooden legs of the table and chairs. And the human legs of his new family.

Hercules particularly liked the look of Jack's legs. They didn't keep still like the others. Jack's legs swung to and fro and his feet wound themselves around each other in interesting knots.

There were long laces too, which hung from Jack's trainers and dangled invitingly in front of Hercules' nose.

21

Hercules tried one of the laces. First he chewed it and made it soggy. Then he gave it a tug. Jack shot his foot out.

'Gerroff,' he snapped, dropping the peas off his fork.

'Sit still at the table, Jack,' said Mum.

'It's the dog!' complained Jack. 'It's eating my Nikes!'

'Don't be silly,' said Dad. He peered under the table at Hercules, who was lying quite still with his chin resting on neatly folded paws.

Jack could feel the thump of a wagging tail against one of his legs. He pulled both legs back and tucked his feet around the chair out of the way.

Dad reached down and gave Hercules a pat. This encouraged the little dog to jump up at the table. He stretched his long body like elastic until his scrappy front paws made contact with the table top.

'You shouldn't let dogs do that,' moaned Jack. 'It's bad manners.'

Mum raised an eyebrow. 'He doesn't understand, Jack. He's just trying to be friendly.' She offered Hercules a titbit

22

from her plate and popped it into the gaping, hairy mouth.

'The poor thing's had a really tough time,' said Dad. 'He's only young, yet he's been very badly treated. His last owner kept him locked up in a shed on the railway allotments twenty-four hours a day. Only kept him to guard his rotten tool-shed. That's why the RSPCA took him away. The poor little fellow needs lots of TLC, don't you, boy?'

Hercules closed one eye as Dad scratched just the right spot behind his left ear.

'What's TLC?' asked Jack, quizzically.

Mum smiled. 'Tender loving care, Jack. TLC.'

Jack pulled a face. 'Yuck!' Hercules had already got both of his parents wrapped around his scruffy, wagging tail.

Well, it won't work with me, thought Jack. He was feeling very determined about this as he excused himself from the table.

Jack decided to take his bike out for

a spin along The Tunnels. The Tunnels was a long, winding grass track, overhung with trees, which snaked its way between the back fields down to the pebble beach at Sandy Spit.

Jack closed the garden gate behind him and set off down the lane. There were some great bends along The Tunnels for doing rear-wheel skids.

Hercules watched Jack disappear in a cloud of dust. Then he squeezed his body, like a tube of toothpaste, through the space between the wooden slats of the gate, and trotted down the lane after his young master.

*   *   *

Down at the beach, Jack was pebble-skimming. Jack's dad was brilliant at this. He could make a single pebble bounce across the waves four or five times before it sank beneath the water. He'd taught Jack how to do it, too. How to hold the flattest pebble you could find with the tips of your fingers, and then throw it sort of sideways, quickly.

24

Jack's first pebble plopped into the water as soon as it touched the surface. But his second one bounded three times before it sank.

As Jack stooped to pick up a third pebble, he heard a scrabble of paws on the shingle and looked up to see Hercules watching him from the ridge.

'What are *you* doing here?' sighed Jack.

'Wuff!' Hercules answered with a soft bark. Then he slid down the shingle ridge on his belly and sat on the stones looking up at Jack. A long pink tongue lolled out of his mouth and one ear was cocked, listening, waiting.

'Go home!' said Jack. 'Go on, shoo!'

But Hercules just barked. 'Wuff! Wuff!'

Jack skimmed the pebble he was holding. One bounce, two, three, four.

'YES!' yelled Jack. He had beaten his own record.

Hercules leaped into the sea and swam after the pebble. He paddled and splashed about in the water where the stone had disappeared.

Hercules waited for another to be

thrown. Jack tossed a big rock lazily
into the sea. It sunk as soon as it hit the
water.

Stupid dog, thought Jack. Then he
picked up a piece of driftwood and

threw it into the waves. The little dog retrieved the stick and swam to the shore with it clamped between his jaws.

But Jack wasn't playing. He hauled his bike up off the beach and swung his leg lazily over the saddle.

As Jack rushed off, Hercules dropped the stick and shook himself dry. Then he watched Jack climb the ridge and ride away.

With a short bark, Hercules followed.

Jack rode his bike as fast as he could back along The Tunnels. He didn't look behind once, even though he knew that Hercules was running as fast as he could to catch up.

Back at the cottage, Jack stashed his bike and went inside. Several minutes later, Hercules came scampering into the kitchen. His claws clicked on the polished floor tiles.

Mum was in the kitchen putting the dishes away. She opened a tin of dog food and spooned the meaty chunks into a brown earthenware dish.

'Put this down for Hercules,' Mum said, smiling at Jack.

Jack gave the little dog his dinner then went off to watch TV. Hercules gobbled the lot hungrily. His mad dash up and down The Tunnels had given him quite an appetite.

That night, as the house slept, Hercules climbed out of his cardboard box next to the Aga and pushed the kitchen door ajar with his nose. Then he stole his way upstairs and curled himself up on the carpet outside Jack's bedroom. door. And there Hercules stayed until morning, guarding his young master.

CHAPTER FOUR

The next morning, after breakfast, Hercules stood at the front door with his new lead in his mouth. Keen eyes shone brightly beneath the scrubbing-brush fringe, and his tail was wagging like crazy

'Perhaps you'd like to take Hercules for a little walk before school,' said Mum.

Jack grunted and said something about not having time. His class was planning a jumble sale at the weekend to raise money for a school trip.

Everyone was going to school half an hour early to help sort out the things for the stalls.

Mum had completely forgotten about the school's fund-raising event. She owned Magpie, a bric-a-brac antique shop in Sallyford, and had said that she would donate some things for Jack to take along.

Jack's mum was always on the look out for a bargain. And her shop was very popular with holidaymakers. Every day, tourists came from Fentown and Rilport on the steam-train excursion. They came to take photographs of the old station, to walk about the picture-postcard village. And to visit the gardens of Cranberry Manor. Others had cream teas at Kettles Tea Garden, and most ended up in Magpie. The tourists were very good for business.

Mrs Singer delved into a cardboard box and produced two lovely hand-painted plates.

'Here you are, Jack. You can ask at least five pounds each for these on your stall.'

She wrapped the plates carefully in newspaper and put them into a plastic carrier bag.

Hercules watched all this with great interest. He cocked his head to one side and looked up at Jack as if to say, 'What about my walk, then?'

'It's no use, Hercules,' said Mum. 'We've got a busy morning today. I'm afraid you'll have to stay at home. Poor old Hercules.' The little dog's ears drooped. His tail dropped and his head went down. Gently, Mum took the lead from him and hung it up.

'You'll have to stay in the kitchen, boy. I'll take you for a walk when I come home for lunch.'

Hercules drooped even more.

Mum glanced at her watch. 'Look at the time, Jack! I'd better hurry. I've got Farmer Dale coming into the shop early this morning to buy that big vase in the window as a birthday present for his wife. Come on, Hercules, kitchen! Help me, Jack.'

Jack took hold of Hercules' collar and pulled him towards the kitchen. Then he gave him a quick push through the door and shut it before Hercules could dodge back out again.

Hercules barked for a few moments. Then he went very quiet.

'I wonder what he's doing in there?' said Mum uneasily. But there was no time to find out. She was already late.

34

She hurried out of the front door with Jack close behind.

*   *   *

As Jack set off for school, Hercules began exploring the kitchen. In all the excitement, the back door hadn't been locked properly.

It only took Hercules a few minutes to discover this. First, he scrabbled at the door with his paws. Then he stretched his long body and reached up to the door handle. Hercules could just about manage to take the handle in his mouth and give it a pull. The handle moved and the door swung open.

Hercules bounded out into the garden and promptly squeezed himself through the wooden slats of the front gate. He reached the top of the lane just in time to see Jack step up on to the school bus.

Hercules watched the bus pull away and head off towards Fentown. He barked twice then trotted off along the country lane in hot pursuit.

Keeping up with the bus was no

35

problem. Being a very determined dog, Hercules had already made up his mind that he was not going to be left behind at any cost. Hercules was going to school!

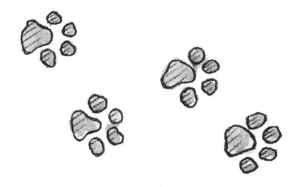

CHAPTER FIVE

No one on the school bus noticed the little dog running along behind. Jack sat in his seat looking straight ahead, clutching the plates his mum had given him for school. Even when the bus pulled up outside the school gates, nobody saw Hercules padding steadily over the rise.

Jack joined the other children in the playground, then went into school.

In Class 4, the air was thick with noise and excitement. All the children were busy unpacking their gifts of jumble and presenting them to the teacher. Mrs Hicks was delighted with the variety of contributions for the sale. She was particularly pleased with Jack's two plates.

'We can ask at least four pounds each for these,' she announced.

'Five,' said Jack. 'My Mum said at least five pounds.'

'Then five pounds it is,' smiled the teacher. She wrote out two price tags and taped them to the plates.

Soon everyone was busy writing and sticking price tags and labels. The whole class was sorting and packing boxes ready to be taken into the storeroom for safekeeping.

'Now, Jack. Take your two plates, and these china bowls along to the storeroom for me,' said Mrs Hicks brightly. 'CJ, you can take these cups and saucers. Just follow Jack and put everything neatly in the empty spaces on the shelves. Off you go. And be careful. We don't want to break anything, do we?'

As Jack set off from the classroom, he suddenly caught a glimpse of

Hercules coming into the school through the outside door at the far end of the corridor. The little dog disappeared into the storeroom as quick as a flash.

'Oh no!' whispered Jack.

'What is it?' asked CJ. She scuffled along close behind, dragging her hobnail boots.

'Nothing,' said Jack. He hurried down the corridor and rushed into the storeroom ahead of her.

Without thinking, Jack yelled, 'Hercules!' And when the little dog looked up he was so excited that he leaped towards Jack with his tail wagging madly.

But Jack was caught off balance. 'Ooops!' gasped Jack. He grabbed at a shelf to steady himself. The shelf was wonky, and a pile of old textbooks fell off it.

Jack tried to save the books but bumped into another shelf instead. This time a stack of china cups came crashing down on to the floor.

At that exact moment, CJ entered the storeroom and Hercules spun

41

round.

CJ screamed in surprise and next moment—another CRASH! as Hercules dodged between CJ's legs and tripped her up.

Down crashed her armful of china, spilling on to the floor in a shattering pile. The noise was terrific.

'Hercules!' yelled Jack. But the loud crash had startled the little dog. He didn't like loud noises at all, and he was off. Dashing out of the storeroom, Hercules shot down the long corridor like a rocket. His paws slipped and skidded on the varnished floor.

The rest of the class, coming along the other way with armfuls of items for the fund-raising sale, met Hercules head on.

As he zoomed past them, things got dropped, spilled and smashed all over the floor. CRASH! SMASH! CRASH! Teachers opened their classroom doors and peered out into the corridor to see what all the noise was about.

One of them, Mr Green, tried to grab Hercules. But Hercules was far too quick and darted through the

teacher's legs and away

To Jack's horror, Mr Green stumbled and knocked a vase of flowers off the windowsill. CRASH! The vase fell and smashed, spilling water and scattering flowers everywhere.

'HERCULES! COME HERE!' yelled Jack. But the runaway dog kept going down the length of the corridor at what seemed like a hundred kilometres an hour.

As Mrs Hicks stepped out of Class 4, a grey blur whizzed past her long skirt and disappeared into the classroom behind her.

Hercules took an enormous leap and landed on a table stacked with ornaments. His claws scrabbled across the polished surface sending everything flying. He cleared the table in two seconds flat.

Then, as Jack burst into the classroom, followed by what seemed like the entire school, Hercules gave a little whimper and lay down on the table with a thud.

The little dog let out a big sigh. Then

he closed his eyes and tried to hide by burying his face beneath two folded paws.

'Hercules, you bad dog!' yelled Jack. He grabbed the little dog's collar before he could shoot off again, and held on firmly. Scattered across the floor were the smashed and broken remains of the carefully labelled ornaments. The donations for the school jumble sale.

Mrs Hicks stood in the doorway with a face like thunder. Suddenly there was a horrible silence. Mrs Hicks was furious. Most of the children peering in from the corridor thought it was all very funny. Some even giggled, and this made the teacher even crosser.

Mr Green produced a length of stout string and tied it securely to Hercules' collar.

'Does anyone know where this animal came from?' he asked grimly.

Jack lowered his eyes and looked down at his trainers. 'I'm afraid he belongs to me, sir,' said Jack. 'But it's not my fault,' he added, 'I don't even know how he got here. I left him at home. He must have got out somehow and followed me.'

'But you live in Sallyford, Jack!' exclaimed Mr Green. 'That's ten kilometres away. Unless this dog took a taxi, I can't see how he could possibly have got here so quickly'

'Well, that really doesn't matter now, does it?' snapped Mrs Hicks. 'The point is that he IS here. And just look at all the damage he's caused. We'll probably have to cancel the jumble sale now. No point in having a fund-raising event with nothing to sell. And that will mean no school trip, I'm afraid.'

Class 4 very quietly sat back at their desks as Mrs Hicks told Jack to take Hercules home. She spoke in a very stern manner and poor Jack felt terrible. He felt responsible for all the damage his stupid dog had caused. And, worst of all, responsible for there being no school trip.

*   *   *

Mrs Hicks rang his mum at the shop and told her that Jack and his dog were

46

being sent home from school in disgrace. His mum would drop him back at lunchtime—*without* Hercules. The rest of the class were already busy clearing up the mess as Jack and Hercules boarded the number twenty-eight bus back to Sallyford.

Hercules didn't seem at all bothered by the fuss and trouble he had caused. He sat on the seat next to Jack wagging his tail for all he was worth. Thump, thump, thump, against Jack's leg.

Hercules licked Jack's hand. And, no matter how rotten Jack felt, he couldn't help smiling. Jack saw Mrs Hicks' face inside his head, like the rerun of a video. He remembered all the crashing and smashing with Hercules darting here and there, and all the teachers trying to catch him. Looking back, it really was quite funny. Jack found himself laughing.

Then, before Jack realised what he was doing, he had flung his arms around Hercules and given him a big hug.

Hercules slobbered all over Jack, licking his rosy cheeks. And Jack found

himself laughing again. The little dog squirmed with delight in Jack's arms. He was so happy.

It was ten o'clock when the bus finally pulled up at Jack's stop.

'Come on, Hercules. Let's go home!'

Jack leaped off the bus with Hercules still tied to the length of string. Hercules didn't seem to mind

48

his makeshift lead and padded along quite happily next to his new master. He looked up at Jack as if to say, 'Are we having our walk now?' And everything was fine until Jack stopped off at Ricketts Bridge, downline from Sallyford Station.

Jack had decided to watch the *Pacific Princess* come through from his favourite spot on the bridge. The old steamer was due at any minute, bringing the first tourists of the day from Rilport.

The excitement of seeing the *Princess* and the noise the train made as she roared along, rattling the wooden bridge when she passed beneath, always thrilled Jack. He loved all the steam, and the smoke, and the shrill scream of the whistle when the engine rumbled through.

But it all proved too much for Hercules. The poor dog was terrified of noisy trains. Having spent so much time locked away in a shed on the railway allotments, only metres away from the tracks and the roaring, rumbling engines, Hercules was scared out of his wits.

A sudden, sharp tug on the string, and Hercules pulled the lead out of Jack's hand. Now he was running for his life along the embankment next to the track. Flying like the wind, Hercules disappeared into the wild brambles and undergrowth of nettles which grew alongside the embankment.

Jack hoped that Hercules was heading towards their cottage and home.

Ricketts Bridge was still trembling with vibrations from the passing steamer as Jack bounded down the wooden steps two at a time.

'Hercules, come back! Hercules, you silly dog, it's only a train. COME BACK!' called Jack. But Hercules had gone.

CHAPTER SIX

Jack cleared the last four steps of the bridge in one leap. The soles of his trainers slapped the concrete paving just as Leading Railman Barnes poked his head through the signalbox window.

Although Sallyford Station was fully computerised, Barney always operated the old hand signals for the holidaymakers when the *Pacific Princess* came in. The tourists like to see things working the old way.

That was how Barney saw Hercules taking off. He had just reset the signal lever and glanced out on to the track. Barney was surprised to see Jack on the bridge. But he was even more surprised to see Jack's dog flying like a rocket, downline, along the embankment.

Barney called out and pointed in the direction that Hercules had taken.

'You'd better hurry, Jack. He's going like a greyhound. Never seen a dog run so fast. Cut right across the siding, he has. Looks like he's heading for the stone quarry.'

'He's probably run home,' Jack yelled back. 'I think the train scared the whiskers off him. He doesn't like the noise.'

Then Jack set off in a hurry, as fast as his legs would carry him, down Railway Lane towards home.

Jack half expected Hercules to be waiting by the front gate of the cottage. But no such luck.

Jack checked the front garden. Then he looked around at the back. He peered beneath the bushes and under the hedges. But there was no Hercules to be seen anywhere.

Then Jack had a sudden thought. It was ten thirty now. Mum was still at Magpie. Perhaps Hercules had found his way to the shop? The little dog seemed capable of anything. Perhaps he'd gone looking for Mum.

Jack put his legs into top gear and ran all the way down the lane and through the village to his mum's shop.

He arrived at Magpie out of breath and red in the face, panting as though he had just finished a marathon.

'What on earth's wrong?' said Mum when Jack burst into the shop. 'And what have you been up to at school? I was very surprised by Mrs Hicks' phone call.'

The door chimes were still tinkling as Jack began to explain. Mum listened carefully to Jack's story. She pulled a face and frowned when she heard about all the damage Hercules had caused at school. But she was full of concern when she heard about the train.

'Right,' Mum said, when Jack had finished. 'I'll lock up the shop and then we'd better go looking for him. The poor thing's probably hiding somewhere half scared out of his wits. I hope he has the sense to keep away from the line!'

Jack's insides suddenly felt as taut as a kite string.

'I don't think Hercules will go anywhere near the line, Mum,' Jack said hopefully. 'He seems to be terrified of trains.'

'It's my fault,' his mum replied. 'I should have checked the kitchen door before we left this morning.' Then she ushered Jack out of the shop and locked the door, after checking it twice.

'I'll walk the embankment, Jack. You look around the village and the fields,' said Mum. 'Look under all the cars and check the old barn in the top meadow. Meet me back at the cottage by eleven thirty. I'll call Dad on the mobile and tell him what's happened. Perhaps he can spare Barney for half an hour.' Mum was really good at organising things. She was brilliant.

Jack smiled and felt a little better. He was almost certain they would find Hercules. It was only a question of time.

First, they checked back at the
cottage again, just in case. But no luck.
Mum picked up Hercules' lead, then
they both split up to search for the
runaway.

The streets and narrow lanes of
Sallyford had suddenly become very

crowded. Tourists from the *Pacific Princess* excursion were milling everywhere.

Jack dodged around the smiling holidaymakers, calling for Hercules and ducking between legs to peer under parked cars. But somehow Jack knew that he was wasting his time. Hercules was a clever dog and would have answered to his name. It was trains that Hercules was afraid of, not people.

Jack decided to leave the village to check the fields and the barn in the top meadow, like Mum had said. Jack walked the fields calling and whistling. Every second he hoped that the little dog would come bounding along wagging his scrappy tail.

Suddenly, there was movement up ahead in the long grass. Something was running for deeper cover towards the hedgerow. Jack's spirits lifted for a moment. But it wasn't Hercules. He could see now that it was only a frightened rabbit diving into its burrow.

The time passed quickly, but despite all of Jack's searching he found nothing. Then Jack thought of The Tunnels. Maybe Hercules had gone down to the beach! He flew back to the cottage to collect his bike.

Jack pedalled furiously and was soon standing on the pebble ridge overlooking the shingle shoreline of Sandy Spit. His keen eyes scanned the coastline, but the beach was deserted.

A tight knot of worry started to gnaw at Jack's stomach and he began to feel a bit sick.

'Hercules, where *are* you?' Jack glanced at his watch. It was coming up to a quarter past eleven.

Jack was just thinking of heading back when he suddenly remembered something Barney had said. Something about Hercules heading for the stone quarry.

Jack didn't waste a second. He pushed his bike on to the flat and took a short cut through the salt marshes, heading in a wide arc away from the coast. Then he pedalled uphill towards the quarry.

When the going became too steep to ride, Jack left his bike and continued

on foot. New hope filled his heart as he reached the edge of the quarry pit.

Please be there, Hercules, thought Jack. *Please, please be there!*

CHAPTER SEVEN

The stone quarry hadn't been worked for years. Jack sometimes went there to search for fossils and rocks for his collection.

Jack knew his way around the maze of pathways, which ran between the gravel pits, like the back of his hand. But the recent dry weather had turned the paths to dusty tracks. Loose stones spilled over into the first two shallow basins that Jack peered into.

A scree of loose stones lay across the pathway which led to the third. Jack's feet slipped and slid, crunching gravel underfoot as he climbed the rocky slope. It was beginning to feel very dangerous.

Jack checked his watch again. It was eleven thirty now, and he was supposed to be back at the cottage. Jack knew that Mum would be wondering where he was. Then he had a sudden thought. Perhaps Mum had found Hercules. Perhaps he was safe and sound back at home.

Jack stood perched on the edge of the pit, wondering what to do, when suddenly he heard a noise. Straining his ears, Jack listened hard. But he heard only the wind and his own shallow breathing. Wait! No. There was another sound. A small yelping cry coming from down in the depths of the pit. Down where the bushes and gorse grew thick in the belly of the quarry.

Jack looked down into the pit. The sides were practically sheer with a drop of about fifteen metres. The bottom was covered in bushes, and littered with old rubbish and junk. Junk that people had dumped there over the years. Jack saw an old mattress and at least two rusty pram frames along with an old bike wheel tangled amongst the weeds.

The yelping came louder now. Then a bark. It was Hercules. Jack knew without a doubt. He'd recognise that sound anywhere.

Hercules was down there, trapped. And Jack knew that, no matter what, he had to rescue him. Suddenly he really cared about that little dog.

Slowly, Jack inched his way forward. He took it carefully, one step at a time, showering gravel into the gaping hole below as he went.

Jack's heart suddenly lurched as the stones beneath his feet gave way. He was falling. Falling and sliding down into the depths of the old stone quarry, with no one except Hercules to hear his cries for help.

Jack hit the bottom of the pit with a hard thump. Luckily, he landed on the old mattress. A sharp pain shot through his ankle and Jack grabbed his foot. The pain made him wince and tears stung at his eyes. Jack tried to

stand up but he couldn't. His ankle gave way beneath him and he sat down heavily

A tatty grey head poked its way out from beneath a bush near the mattress and licked Jack's hand. It was Hercules. The little dog looked up at Jack and gave a pathetic whine. And Jack's heart melted.

He could see that the string tied to Hercules' collar was caught on one of the pram frames. The little dog must have tumbled into the quarry pit and got himself trapped.

Jack quickly untied the string and set Hercules free. The little dog yapped and barked as he danced around Jack, his tail wagging as if to say, 'I'm OK now. Come on, let's go!'

But Jack couldn't go. Jack couldn't move. And no one knew he was there.

Hercules bounced and bounded at Jack's feet. He dived and chewed Jack's loose laces, eager for a game. Then he attacked the old mattress Jack was lying on. Great tufts of wadding flew into the air. The little dog seemed so happy, he couldn't understand why his new master was just lying there.

Jack rubbed his sore ankle and winced with pain.

'Ow! I think it's badly twisted,' he muttered to himself.

Hercules leaped on to Jack's lap and began licking his face vigorously

Even though Jack's ankle was hurting like crazy, he grinned at the little scrappy bundle of fur. Suddenly it was as if Jack had owned Hercules all his life. And he loved him to pieces.

Jack gave Hercules a big hug and ruffled his floppy ears.

'I'm sorry I was so rotten to you,' he said.

Hercules gave his 'no problem' answer with a soft bark. 'Wuff, wuff.' His tail wagged excitedly as he cocked his head to one side and looked up into Jack's face.

'I can't move, boy!' began Jack. 'My ankle's twisted and there's no way I can climb out of here.'

The little dog seemed to be listening to every word that Jack said. He pricked up his ears and his eyes lit up with anticipation.

The sides of the quarry were very steep. And, as Jack peered up to the rocky summit, he suddenly realised how impossible it would be for either himself or Hercules to climb out.

But Jack didn't know how determined Hercules could be once he'd made up his mind to do something.

It took a little time, but, once Hercules realised that his master was in trouble, there was no stopping him.

First, the little dog peered up to the sky, studying the outline of rock which marked the top of the quarry pit. Hercules scurried around on his stumpy legs, then gave a series of little hops and leaps as he investigated the quarry basin.

Suddenly, his keen eyes followed a rocky ledge which wound its way round and down into the quarry. A narrow ledge which spiralled both downwards from the summit of the pit, and led upwards, to freedom.

Hercules gave a sharp bark and scraped at Jack's leg with his paw. His tail thumped the mattress noisily.

Hercules was trying to tell Jack that he had seen a way out.

'Wuff! Wuff!' his soft bark echoed off the stone walls.

'What is it, boy?' Jack followed Hercules' gaze. Then he noticed the narrow ledge, too.

'I don't think so,' said Jack, 'Even if my foot was OK, I'd never climb that! It's far too narrow.'

But Hercules didn't think so. Not for him, anyway. He may have looked fat and dumpy to Jack, but surprisingly Hercules was an athlete of a dog. He would scale the sheer rock face if he had to. The narrow ledge, however dangerous it looked, made it easy-peasy. Hercules was going to get out. And get help for Jack.

CHAPTER EIGHT

Circling the quarry pit, Hercules snuffled and scrabbled through the long grass and bushes which grew there. He was looking for a way up on to the first part of the ledge.

Jack watched as the little hero stretched his body like elastic, and tried to reach up with his scrappy paws.

'Hang on, Hercules,' said Jack. 'I'll crawl over and give you a hand.'

But the little dog had already bunched up his muscles and leaped. Two determined front paws clamped on to the ledge. And two equally determined hindlegs scratched and scrabbled at the stone wall until they settled Hercules safely on the first part of the escape route.

'*Yes!*' cried Jack. He punched the air and called out to his athletic scamp. 'Well done, boy. Well done, Hercules!'

'Wuff, wuff.' Hercules thumped the rocky shelf with his tail and sent a cloud of dust and stones flying as he scampered off along the ledge.

Jack watched him go round and round the walls of the pit. 'Go on, boy. Good dog,' he called out encouragingly.

And, with each circuit, Hercules climbed higher and higher.

'Be careful, boy' At one point Jack held his breath. The ledge became dangerously narrow and loose stones spilled over the edge and rained down into the pit and on to Jack's head.

Hercules went down on to his belly and slowly scrabbled forward, inching his way along a paw length at a time. One side of his whiskers brushed the quarry wall. The other side hung over the edge with nothing but a sheer drop

below.

Hercules gave a frightened whine.

'Be careful, boy,' cried Jack. 'You're almost there. You can do it!'

Hercules crawled forward, like a snake on his belly, until the ledge became wide enough again for him to stand. Then he was off like a rocket. He zoomed around the last stretch at about two hundred kilometres an hour.

Suddenly Jack gasped. He'd noticed a big crack along the final length of the ledge. A huge gap in the rocky path that Hercules was bounding along.

'Hercules!' yelled Jack. 'Watch out!' Jack bit his bottom lip and hoped the little dog had seen the gap.

But Hercules' eye-level was very low on the ground, and he was still racing along as though his life depended on it.

'No, Hercules! Stop! *Stop!*' Jack cried. His voice echoed around the pit.

But it was too late. Suddenly the gaping crack was there. And so was Hercules.

With a surprised yelp and a brilliant leap, the little dog sailed over the broken ledge.

The crack was at least two metres across, but luckily Hercules was travelling fast enough to breach the gap.

But he landed badly with a thump and a roll in a mad scrabble of dust, paws and loose stones. To Jack, it looked as if Hercules was about to fall off the ledge. But something hard and

solid, like a pipe or a stick, poked out
from the quarry wall. And Hercules
managed to clamp his jaws around it
and hold on tight. His hindlegs slipped
over the ledge and he was left hanging;
dangling in the air. But his jaws held
fast.

For a moment Jack's heart missed a
beat, then he punched the sky with
both fists in a cry of triumph as the
little dog pulled himself up, with a mad

scrabble of paws.

'*Yes!!* Hercules, you did it!'

Once safely back up the ledge, Hercules called down to Jack with a series of sharp barks.

He was only a short hop away now from being out of the pit.

'Attaboy, Hercules,' yelled Jack. 'Go and fetch help. Bring help!'

The little dog peered down over the edge from the rocky summit. He gave a low whimper followed by a series of excited barks. 'Wuff, wuff, wuff!'

Then he turned on his heels and ran off through the quarry towards the village, on a mission to get help for Jack.

Hercules ran as fast as his little legs would carry him, kicking up stones all along the gravel path on his way down the hill.

He stopped, for the briefest of seconds, when he passed Jack's bike stashed against a rock. Then he was off again, across the salt marshes, heading for the railway track.

CHAPTER NINE

Hercules didn't like trains. He didn't like trains at all. In fact, the noise that trains made terrified him. All those months locked away in a shed on the railway allotments had turned brave Hercules into a very nervous hero.

But to get back to the village and bring help, Hercules first had to cross the Sallyford railway line.

The little dog whimpered quietly to himself as he climbed the embankment on shaky legs. His nose twitched and trembled as he smelled the diesel, the wooden sleepers and the scent of trains.

Hercules grumbled a nervous growl from deep in his throat. Suddenly his ears flattened against his head and he sank down on to his belly between the tracks. Hercules' legs had turned to jelly just as the twelve o'clock Rilport Express was about to thunder through on the Sallyford line.

Hercules was frozen to the spot. He buried his head beneath two folded paws and tried to flatten himself into the gravel chippings on the track.

Hercules closed his eyes and felt the vibrations of the train rumbling along the line. The noise became deafening as the express roared nearer and nearer.

Hercules dared to peek. He opened one eye and peered through his wiry scrubbing-brush fringe at the huge black train which was bearing down and about to squash him.

Hercules tightly clamped his eyes shut again, and thought of Jack.

The Rilport Express sounded its horn with a long, droning blast, as it roared only metres away from the little dog.

Suddenly Hercules found his legs again, along with his courage. A picture of his young master filled his doggy thoughts and he sprang from the track only seconds before the engine and carriages flew past with their deafening clickety-clack chorus.

Hercules sat tall on the other side of the track.

Clickety clack. Clickety clack. Clickety clack. The noisy train passed centimetres from his whiskers. But Hercules sat fast and didn't move. His little body quivered and trembled with fright, but he sat tight until the Express had passed.

Hercules now knew that the trains wouldn't hurt him. Like noisy dogs, sometimes their bark was worse than their bite. But he would always be wary of the noisy engines and the rickety tracks on which they tore about. Trains would always be treated with caution, like cats.

The Express disappeared into a distant tunnel as Hercules turned and ran down into the village.

*   *   *

Jack's mum was at the cottage worrying. She checked her watch for the umpteenth time. It was ten past twelve.

'Jack should have been here forty minutes ago,' she exclaimed aloud. 'Something's happened. I know it has!'

She picked up the telephone and was just about to phone Mr Singer again on his mobile when she heard a scraping sound at the back door.

'Jack!' Mrs Singer rushed to the door and pulled it open. To her surprise, a little scruffy bundle of dusty fur burst into the kitchen. It was Hercules, his claws clicking on the polished floor tiles. The little dog wiggled and wagged his tail for all he was worth. Then he started barking—and he wouldn't stop. Mum knew straight away that Hercules was trying to tell her something.

'It's Jack, isn't it?' she said quickly. 'Where is he, Hercules?' She noticed that the little dog's fur was covered in grey dust.

Hercules stretched out his forepaws and looked up at Mum with wide, wide

eyes.

'Take me to him,' said Mum. 'You can take me to him, can't you?'

'Wuff, wuff, wuff!'

She clipped Hercules' lead on to his collar, then quickly called her husband on his mobile.

'Meet me at the end of the lane in five minutes,' said Mum. 'It's Jack.

Something's happened. I've got Hercules here. He came home on his own, but he's covered in grey dust as though he's been rolling in gravel.'

'The quarry,' said Mr Singer immediately. 'It's got to be. I'll bring a rope and meet you there in five minutes!'

CHAPTER TEN

Hercules strained on his lead and pulled Mum along the lane, over the track and through the salt marshes. Dad trotted along behind with a thick coil of rope over his shoulder.

The climb up the hill to the quarry pits had them both huffing and puffing. But Hercules was full of stamina and just kept on going.

They found Jack's bike and Mum started calling. 'Jack! Jack! Can you hear us?'

Her voice was lost on the wind. But

Hercules' barking carried a message of hope which filtered down into the quarry pit.

Jack lifted his head. 'Yes!' He could hear barking. It was Hercules. He'd come back with help.

'Here!' he yelled at the top of his voice. 'I'm over here!'

Mum, Dad and Hercules peered over the edge of the quarry down into the pit.

Hercules threw back his head and howled.

'Jack,' cried his mum. 'Are you all right?'

Jack looked up at his parents. 'It's my ankle,' he called. 'I think it's twisted. I can't walk.'

Mum had to hang on tightly to Hercules' lead to stop him leaping into the pit to be with Jack.

Dad looked around for something to tie the end of his rope to. He peered over the edge and down the sheer sides of the quarry pit.

The stick which had saved Hercules earlier stuck out from the ledge. Dad saw it and bent down to test its strength.

'It seems solid enough,' he said, giving it a hard yank. He tied the rope around it with a double knot and took a deep breath. Slowly, using the length of rope, he lowered himself down the sheer face of the quarry wall. The narrow ledges became footholds as he slid down the rocky wall to rescue Jack.

Hercules strained to reach forward and help, but there was no more the little dog could do. He had brought help, and now he just had to watch and

wait.

Down in the quarry pit, Dad lifted Jack on to his back, turned around and slowly hauled himself back up the quarry face.

*   *   *

Hercules went berserk when he saw Jack. The little dog barked and leaped up at Dad, trying to lick his master's face. But all he could reach was Jack's feet.

Although he was in pain with his ankle, Jack laughed as Hercules pulled off one of his trainers, and ran in circles with it.

'Hercules, give that back!' said Mum sternly.

The little dog dropped it immediately, then watched it roll over the edge and into the gravel pit.

'Oh, no!' moaned Mum. She peered over to see where the trainer had fallen. Luckily it was lying only a metre or so away, on the ledge below.

As Mum knelt to retrieve Jack's shoe, she suddenly noticed the stick which Dad had tied the rope to. Only it wasn't a stick at all. And it wasn't an old pipe, either. It was some kind of metal handle. And it was engraved with a very distinctive design.

'Hey, Dad,' called Mum. 'Come over here and take a look at this.'

'Go on, Dad,' said Jack. 'I'm all right. I'll just sit down here while you go and have a look.'

Mum gave Jack's trainer to Hercules. 'Here, hold this for a minute.' The little dog clamped his fuzzy jaws around the shoe and sat down with a thump beside Jack. Then he watched Mum and Dad investigate the funny stick he had found.

'This pattern is definitely Celtic,' announced Mum. 'And I think it's a bronze handle.'

'What kind of a handle?' asked Dad.

'The handle of a sword,' exclaimed Mum. 'A Celtic one.'

'What's going on?' called Jack. 'What have you found over there?'

Dad scrabbled away at the loose rock where the handle seemed to enter the quarry wall. Stone crumbled and fell away as he worked.

'It's not just a handle,' said Dad. 'It's a whole sword!' He gradually managed to pull it out from its stone scabbard— the crack in the wall where the sword had been buried for hundreds of years.

'Jack hobbled over. 'Wow!' he whistled through his teeth. 'Can we keep it?'

'I don't think so,' smiled Dad. He lay the sword on the grass for everyone to see. 'The quarry's on Farmer Dale's land,' he added, 'so it really belongs to him.'

'You just leave Farmer Dale to me,' said Jack's mum. 'He owes me a big favour. And when I tell him about my plans for this sword he won't be able to refuse.'

Jack looked up at Dad with a puzzled frown. But Dad had no idea what Mum was up to, either.

'Who's a clever dog, then?' smiled Mum as she bent down to scratch Hercules between the ears.

'Yes!' said Jack. He suddenly remembered that it had been Hercules who had discovered the sword.

'Hercules has been brilliant.'

Hercules stopped growling at the ancient sword and bounced up on to his hindlegs. He rested his front paws on Jack's legs, looked up at him adoringly and gave a soft wuffling grumble.

Jack forgot his bad ankle and gave Hercules a huge hug. At last he realised how special the dog was. He'd only owned him a few days, but he was beginning to realise that life would never be the same again. In fact, he couldn't imagine being without the scruffy little dog.

Jack linked his arm through his dad's and half-hobbled, half-walked down the gravel path and out of the quarry. When they got to Jack's bike, Dad lifted him into the saddle and steered him all the way back home, freewheeling along the country lanes, Hercules happily trotting alongside, Mum following close behind clutching his amazing find—the antique Celtic sword.

CHAPTER ELEVEN

Back at the cottage, Mum called Dr Kelham, who came over straight away to check Jack's ankle.

'It's just a mild sprain,' said the doctor. He bandaged Jack's foot and told him not to run around on it for a day or two.

'Can I still exercise Hercules?' Jack asked, pleadingly.

'So long as you take it nice and easy,' warned the doctor. 'No galloping along like a madman!'

'I can ride my bike,' grinned Jack.

'Hercules can do all the galloping. He's really fast!'

Hercules leaped up and smothered Jack with slobbering licks.

While they were talking, Mum slipped away and telephoned Farmer Dale. And, judging by the big grin on her face when she put the receiver down, she had persuaded him to let her do whatever she liked with the Celtic sword.

One week later, Mum turned up at Jack's school with Hercules. The little dog was very well behaved, and sat beside Mum, as good as gold, while she spoke to Jack's teacher.

Mrs Hicks eyed Hercules suspiciously as Mrs Singer explained the reason for her visit to the whole class.

'As you know,' she began, 'Hercules here paid a visit to the school last week and caused a spot of damage.'

The teacher raised an eyebrow. 'It was more than a spot!' she said. 'We were hoping to raise enough money to sponsor a school trip—*before* Hercules arrived.'

Mum smiled. 'Well, the good news is, the trip can still go ahead. Hercules found something the other day which was worth quite a bit of money. And we want to use that money to pay for all the damage he caused, and to

finance the school trip, as planned.'

Mrs Hicks smiled. A big bright smile. Jack's face lit up like a Christmas tree. And Hercules launched himself across the desks to lick as many rosy cheeks as he could find. Suddenly, the little hero with the big name had more friends than he realised. And the best friend he could ever have was Jack.